The New Jerusalem

By Yerusalem Work

Copyright © 2016, 2017 by Yerusalem Work

ISBN: 978-1-520-10042-5

All rights reserved. No part of this book may be reproduced or transmitted in any form or by any means, electronic or mechanical, including photocopying, recording, or by any information storage and retrieval system, without permission in writing from the copyright owner.

This book was printed in the United States of America.

At the second annual interfaith picnic in Annandale, VA, Muslims, Christians and Jews congregate for a festive afternoon of unity and kindhearted dialogue. Red, white and blue balloons, plates and utensils decorate the shaded picnic area in this spacious Heartland Park. A couple hundred people gather to experience international cuisine at this neighborly potluck. The scent of doro wat (chicken stew) from Ethiopia, lamb kabobs from Afghanistan and the smell of kosher hamburgers and hot dogs fill everyone's noses. Baba ghanoush (eggplant), grilled vegetables, samosas, hummus with pita bread, falafel salads with tahini dressing and an array of fresh fruit are also popular selections. Parents wipe their adventurous children's faces with napkins. There is something new for everyone.

The bees buzz by the food and hover over the covered trays, as if to supervise. In the August heat, Afghan girls in princess dresses play together by the delicious desserts, rice pudding and baklava. Greek and Ethiopian Orthodox Christians exchange polite greetings and discuss family life. The boys are enjoying a game of soccer. The young women dressed modestly are tossing around neon-colored Frisbees. The young men are playing with their hacky sacks designed in the colors of various national flags from the Middle East, Africa and North America. Out of respect for Islamic tradition, women entertain themselves separately from the men. The children divided by gender move fearlessly in the ferocious sun. Many of the adults have donned national dress from Saudi Arabia, Morocco, Palestine, Afghanistan, Ethiopia, Nigeria and more. Women in pastel-colored hijab are tending to their children and engaging in lively conversation with each other. Not a moment passes without a laugh.

Churches, synagogues and mosques in the Washington, DC, metropolitan area organized this event to introduce the community to the diversity within each sacred gathering place. A pastor in a white long-sleeved polo and blue jeans speaks into the microphone and thanks everyone for attending. This brief speech creates a sense of calm after a half-hour long buffet and a period of boisterous activities soon to resume. The rabbi with his distinctive kippah introduces the importance of interfaith dialogue and social justice. He encourages everyone to meet someone from a different house of worship. An imam wearing a white galabiyya (men's Islamic dress) takes an opportunity to quote the Qur'an in which Allah speaks: “O mankind! We created you from a single (pair) of a male and a female, and made you into nations and tribes, that ye may know each other (not that ye may despise (each other))…(Qur’an 49:13).” These inspiring words build solidarity as people come together for the same purpose: to get to know each other.

Jerusalem, a young Ethiopian librarian with cocoa-colored skin, arrives with a box of pastries. She is melting in the sun, but the pastries land on the dessert table where they are instantly devoured by a swarm of children. Jerusalem and her boyfriend Yohannes (John) drove separately. He followed her to the picnic spot. They notice that men and women are sitting separately as they do at the Ethiopian Orthodox Church. So, without saying a word they mingle with the appropriate crowd. John takes a 2-liter bottle of soda with him to the men’s section. He quickly ingratiates himself to the young men his age by shaking hands and discussing sports and politics. Jerusalem brushes her curly hair off her face and then the wind picks up alleviating her of the task. Birds call to each other and fly in different directions as if carrying messages from treetop to treetop.

The adults shield themselves from the warmth of the sun. A Saudi family enters the picnic grounds in a big, air-conditioned van. The twelve year-old girl, Hawa, follows her mom, Khadijah, to the women's area. Khadijah is wrapped in an olive green abaya with gold embroidery. Hawa's dad, Maaz, a diplomat, beelines to the men's section. His stomach is doing the talking. He gently elbows a neighbor, who is quietly waiting in line for Kabsa (chicken, rice, mixed vegetables, and spices).

Maaz exclaims, “The food last year was great! I brought an appetite.”

His neighbor’s face lights up as he replies, “I did, too!”

Jerusalem acquaints herself with the diplomat’s wife, Khadijah, who is delicate. Khadijah covered in her hijab briskly walks out of the sun and into the shaded picnic area.

Khadijah begins the conversation by proclaiming, “On the Day of Judgment, we’ll only have the shade of the Qur’an.”

Hawa is wearing a fire-engine red hijab with tiny white polka dots. She loves to stand out. She is the youngest of three children. Her two older sisters are both in college out-of-state.

Jerusalem confides that she has read the Qur'an in English and hopes to read it in Arabic soon. Khadijah offers to teach Jerusalem Arabic.

"What can I do in exchange?" Jerusalem wonders aloud. "I teach ballet and modern dance at my parents' church. May I teach concert dance in the Muslim community? Is dance an accepted art form among Muslims? Or is dance strictly prohibited in Islam?"

Hawa, a middle school student born in the U.S., is taller than her petite mother. Hawa places her hand on her mother's shoulder and peers into Jerusalem's eyes as she pleads, "Mom, I want to study ballet."

Her enthusiasm is contagious.

Khadijah insists that Jerusalem teach her daughter ballet.

“Will you give my daughter private ballet lessons? Dance is permissible, as long as you follow certain guidelines. For example, don’t mix genders. Agreed?”

“Yes!” Jerusalem jumps at the chance. Then she reconsiders. Jerusalem, petrified, does not understand if “private ballet lessons” involve working in someone’s home. She had heard of domestic workers in Saudi Arabia being treated unfairly. It is a sensitive subject, so she silences herself.

Jerusalem’s face flushes as she sees John handpick a flower and deliver it to a Methodist woman whose blond hair flows down the length of her back. The Protestant Christian woman refuses his gift. Jerusalem frowns at Johnny and points to her car so they can meet there to have a private conversation. John does not know how to cover his mistake.

"You have a wandering eye," Jerusalem scolds. Jerusalem is hotter than the sun at this point.

Jerusalem's eyes water as she accuses Johnny, "You've never bought me flowers. Do you care about me?" She is angry.

Johnny argues, "Yes, but I don't want to be your boyfriend. If you're not happy with me, I'll leave."

John takes his keys out of his pockets and leaves this family-friendly environment to hang out with his guy friends at a coffee shop. He departs with a blessing, "I hope you find someone who will make you happy. Enjoy the falafels and grape leaves."

Jerusalem's hands are shaking as John's car is automatically unlocked and he drives off. She is mortified. Khadijah brings a napkin to Jerusalem who wipes away her tears. "Don't let your heart break. I'll be your friend. There are no boyfriends in Islam," Khadijah consoles in a mothering tone.

Jerusalem pulls her hair back into a ponytail. "But, I'm Christian. I need a prayer."

Khadijah offers to teach Jerusalem prayers in Arabic. They agree to meet in a week. Jerusalem is Christian, but she is drawn to Classical Arabic, so she intends to study the Qur'an. When her heart breaks, she reads the Qur'an to find peace. "Certainly, the help of Allah is near (Qur'an 2:214)." She remembers reading this verse and etching it onto her heart. After breaking up with her boyfriend, Jerusalem feels she can only seek refuge with Allah.

As Jerusalem's heart heals, Khadijah calls Jerusalem to say, "I love you only for the sake of Allah. You should love only for the sake of Allah."

Jerusalem is still discovering the meaning of love. If there's anything she loves, it's dance. It keeps you young, healthy and happy. Jerusalem wants to love what Allah loves and hate what Allah hates. She asks herself, "Does Allah love when we dance?" She struggles to answer this question.

A week after the interfaith picnic, Khadijah and Jerusalem meet at the park again, but this time alone. They sit at an empty picnic table. This is where Jerusalem will receive a new start by studying Arabic. Khadijah brings a copy of the Qur'an in both English and Arabic. Jerusalem's notebook soon fills with Arabic letters. She pieces the word Allah together and immediately learns a prayer in Arabic from a Surah (chapter) that is equivalent to one-third of the entire Qur'an. She smiles as she breathes deeply. The wind carries the scent of jasmine from the beautiful flowers planted nearby. Khadijah drinks her water. Khadijah offers Jerusalem bottled water. Jerusalem accepts and begins to sip her drink.

"Hold my hands," Khadijah gently asks from across the table. Jerusalem listens to her teacher and holds her hands. Khadijah continues, "Please repeat after me. La ilaha il-Allah; Muhammad ur-Rasool Allah."

Jerusalem repeats slowly every Arabic syllable. Jerusalem has no idea what she just said, but she is caught up in the moment. She is proud, because she thinks she made a complete sentence in Arabic.

Khadijah rejoices, "Now you're Muslim!" The words Jerusalem repeated are the words of the Shahadah, the first confession of a Muslim. In English, the translation is “There is no God but Allah; Muhammad is the Messenger of Allah.”

Now this is a surprise. Jerusalem believes what she reads in the Qur’an, but she doesn’t have any Muslim friends her age. Who will teach her about Islam? Jerusalem is so happy to have at least one new friend, Khadijah. While Khadijah is married with children, Jerusalem is single with no children. Jerusalem submits a silent prayer. She hopes that she will not be expected to start a family. She does not want to marry after her most recent heartbreak. She wants to be a teacher and a librarian, not a mother and a wife. The joy of having a profession is enough. Jerusalem announces, “Becoming Muslim isn’t as complicated as I expected!”

The birds flutter their wings. Jerusalem feels as free as the birds. She thanks Allah for giving her a hand to hold through the conversion process. He is All-Knowing and All-Wise. Jerusalem does not know what to do, but she feels she is transforming into a new woman – the new Jerusalem. A butterfly with purple wings lands on the table and Jerusalem remembers that transformation is a part of everyone's life. Even creatures in nature transform. And oh, how the world transformed after the miracle of the Qur'an. Jerusalem remembers visiting the Alhambra in Spain after college and seeing the majestic architecture. At the Alhambra, she first felt the spirit of Islam. Jerusalem accepts her destiny as a convert and quickly Khadijah becomes her new best friend through this conversion process. It is time for Jerusalem to cover her hair with a headscarf or hijab.

“Let’s go hijab shopping!” Khadijah says enthused as she leads Jerusalem to a nearby mosque where they sell Islamic dress.

Jerusalem follows in a separate car and wonders aloud, “What will happen next?”

As they look through the Islamic clothing selection, Khadijah introduces Jerusalem to the women of the mosque who bless Jerusalem and tell her, “All your past sins are forgiven after you take your Shahadah.”

Khadijah invites Jerusalem to her home and she offers to teach her how to pray. Jerusalem is so excited to visit the home of a diplomat. She hopes to learn how to pray, so she can practice her Arabic. She doesn’t have other Arabic speaking friends, but Allah is her closest Friend. She trusts that she can speak both English and

Arabic in prayer, because Allah understands all. When Khadijah and Jerusalem see Hawa at home, Hawa is texting a friend on her cell phone. Khadijah shares the good news.

"Guess what, honey! Jerusalem took her Shahadah at the park." Khadijah is proud of Jerusalem, who quickly becomes like family.

"I'm Muslim!" Jerusalem then rejoices. She is wearing a black abaya and a brown hijab with gold pattern from Saudi Arabia, which she picked up from the mosque. Immediately, Jerusalem sits with Hawa and tells her, "When I was your age, we did not have cell phones."

Hawa cannot imagine life without her cell phone. How else would everyone stay connected? Cell phones are like veins and arteries. They keep the flow of conversation going. Khadijah asks Hawa to put her cell phone away.

"I can give you your first ballet lesson," Jerusalem promises. The Saudi family's home contains framed wall hangings with Arabic phrases in gold, silver and black. It is an elegant home where you can hear the Adhan (the call to prayer) five times a day from an app saved on the family's iPad. They embrace technology, but they keep their focus on Allah.

This evening Jerusalem devotes a brief thirty minutes to provide an introduction to ballet course for Hawa. Both young women are in hijab. Khadijah runs to the kitchen to prepare dinner. Jerusalem teaches Hawa the five basic hand positions. Then she shows her how to move her feet from first position to sixth position. She demonstrates a *plié* as a simple bend of the knee. Hawa has trouble with turning her legs out from her hips. Her legs are a little shaky. Jerusalem guides her through some exercises to strengthen her inner thighs. Then they stretch their whole bodies, including their hamstrings to increase flexibility.

Hawa enjoys ballet and she is very elegant in her upper body movement, like a princess. Jerusalem is proud of her student as they study themselves in the full-length hallway mirror. Next she'll teach Hawa *dégagés* and *frappés*. They do not have a ballet barre, so they rely on their tummy muscles to keep them firmly in place, like a tree planted in the forest. After working up an appetite, the girls ask Khadijah if dinner is ready. They all drink bottled water and eat a delicious meal with salad, couscous, raisins, vegetables and hummus with pita bread. Khadijah also warmed up lightly seasoned chicken. Hawa wants to slim down with ballet and she will.

The next day at school Hawa walks with greater confidence. Her friends notice her back straight and her body poised. Where does this confidence come from?

“Ballet,” Hawa says. “I’m studying ballet.”

Her friends ask where she is taking classes.

“At my house,” Hawa boasts, “I have a private tutor.”

“Maybe she can teach us, too.”

The girls immediately spin like ballerinas in their long, flowing skirts. After school, Hawa’s friends join her at her house where Jerusalem will stop by in the evening. Hawa asks her mom if Jerusalem can teach her friends ballet. Far from disapproval, the young Muslimahs in the community are keen to study ballet and wear their hijab in the process. Khadijah texts Jerusalem and informs her that there is growing demand in her ballet lessons. Jerusalem responds that she loves the idea of teaching the girls ballet.

"But no boys allowed!" Jerusalem demands. Khadijah agrees wholeheartedly. Jerusalem meets Hawa's friends, Aisha and Salwa. To warm up, the girls do several *grand pliés* and then sit in the splits. Then the girls dive into a ballet lesson. Today Jerusalem teaches the girls the art of spotting, so they can do *pirouttes* and *piqué turns*. Aisha and Salwa get dizzy, but Hawa can keep up with Jerusalem. They are dancing to the sound of Jerusalem's voice as she counts the rhythm: 1 and a 2 and a 3… Aisha, the most energetic, darts in every direction, like a firecracker. Salwa, the skinniest, stands tall, like a camel. Hawa, the most graceful, glides across the floor with elegance. Jerusalem promises to teach them leaps tomorrow. The ballet lesson ends with a selfie of the girls.

Friday comes. It's Jummah.

"Jummah Mubarak!" Khadijah calls out to Jerusalem at the mosque parking lot as they attend a khutbah (Islamic sermon). The news has spread among the women that Jerusalem, a new convert, is teaching some girls ballet. There is quite a buzz. After the ladies pray, a few mothers approach Jerusalem with the hope that their daughters can join the ballet class.

"My daughter wants to study ballet with you," Zahara, a Palestinian mother in designer hijab, expresses intently as she grasps Jerusalem's hand. The class is getting too big to fit in Khadijah's home.

Jerusalem comforts Zahara by saying, "I'd be happy to teach your daughter. Let me find a studio that can host us."

"This ballet class is growing," Jerusalem says to Khadijah on the way home. Jerusalem has the Friday off from the special library where she works. When she returns to the office Monday, Jerusalem researches local ballet schools and calls one to rent a studio one night a week. The school agrees and Jerusalem begins to teach Wednesday nights, but she does not stop at ballet. She explains to the girls that ballet gives us the basic vocabulary to do many forms of dance, including modern, postmodern, jazz and African dance. So the journey begins. She calls the class "The New Jerusalem," because she is honoring her conversion process and how she is turning over a new leaf. "No boyfriends!" she writes in her thought diary. She learned her lesson at the picnic. Goodbye to the old Jerusalem and hello to the new Jerusalem.

The community hears about this new dance class with a combination of ballet, modern, postmodern, jazz and African dance. So, the young people from the interfaith picnic are the first to sign up. Shalom! Salaam! Selam! Hello! Peace! Jerusalem writes greetings on a sign and the girls come together to learn how to dance and to make new friends. Dinah and Sarah, two Reform Jews; Susan, a Korean Baptist; and Dora, a Greek Orthodox Christian, attend the first class in the new studio along with Hawa, Aisha, Salwa and Zahara's daughter, Fatima.

Today Jerusalem teaches them leaps. As they *grand jeté* across the floor, the girls cheer each other on.

"Weeerk!" One of them yells. Aisha and Hawa want to be professional dancers and they give each move their all. The Muslim girls are wearing hijab, but the Christians and Jews are also modestly dressed. When the girls have built up their dance vocabulary, Jerusalem adds Davidic dance to the choreographed movement with its jumps and turns. The students dance in a circle to Hebrew music. Jerusalem also teaches the girls Greek dance, so they can hold hands and dance in a circle. The mothers watch through the window and marvel at how the dancers are in harmony with each other. There is no competition. Everyone does her best and Jerusalem is proud of the camaraderie.

Khadijah asks Jerusalem, "Can the girls put on a performance with costumes?"

Jerusalem is thrilled at this opportunity to show off the students' success. Jerusalem plans to put on a dance concert in six weeks. The girls squeal when they hear about putting on a show.

Jerusalem calls a famous hotel to reserve a ballroom, "May I reserve the Grand Ballroom?"

The hotel schedules the performance. The dancers want to see their costumes.

"What will our costumes look like, Ms. Jerusalem?" Jerusalem asks each girl to wear solid colors – a long-sleeved red t-shirt and a long black skirt. The Muslim girls are asked to wear red hijab.

"We'll all cover our hair," the non-Muslim students agree in solidarity.

A week after the performance is announced the girls come together to shop for dance shoes: ballet slippers and jazz shoes. The store is so happy to see so many new faces. Everyone is a dancer at heart. What Jerusalem teaches the students is that every day is filled with dance. From putting on your socks and shoes to making a peanut butter and jelly sandwich, the world is filled with dance opportunities. You don't have to wear ballet slippers to be considered a dancer.

The performance is called "Night and Day," because Allah transforms night to day and vice versa. The girls perform to Sami Yusuf, Maher Zain and Harris J's music. They move gracefully using their basic dance vocabulary of leg extensions, *pirouettes* and *grand jetés*. Khadijah films her daughter doing a *développé* side, an arabesque, and a *pas de chat.* Then Hawa begins to *chassé* off-stage. Next, the entire group of dancers comes together to share center stage for Greek dance and they close the production with a Davidic dance finale.

The audience gives a standing ovation. All of the moms come together after the show to give flowers to their children who performed. Khadijah gives a single rose to Jerusalem to say thank you. Jerusalem does not have children of her own, but she feels as if these dancers are in essence her own flesh and blood.

"You work so well with the children. You'd be a great mom," Khadijah says with her hand on her heart.

Jerusalem beams a smile and hugs the dancers as she says, "Thank you to the daughters of Jerusalem. You make performing fun and simple."

The daughters of Jerusalem shout in unison, "We love you, Ms. Jerusalem!"

Jerusalem feels a tear stream down her face. As her eyes cool, she replies, “I love you, too!”

At the interfaith picnic, Jerusalem cried very different tears. Her anger has finally cooled. The acceptance from her new community fills her heart with happiness. Could she be the same person whom John left behind, ending their disaster of a relationship? Allah blesses Jerusalem through Khadijah’s friendship. No man has ever expressed his love to Jerusalem, but for the first time, after weeks of building solidarity among young women, Jerusalem loves herself.

Epilogue

“The New Jerusalem” is based on a true story. The seven conditions were not met for the Shahadah or declaration of faith, the first pillar in Islam, but the experience touched the heart and led toward deeper knowledge of Islam. Please carefully study and research a religion before you convert or revert. May God guide you and bless you as you pursue peace.

Life is beautiful
Hear the applause of heaven
when we become friends

Made in the USA
Middletown, DE
21 June 2023